W9-CZN-749

The Future of TECHNOLOGY

What Is the Future of
Virtual Reality?

Carla Mooney

ReferencePoint
Press®

San Diego, CA

© 2017 ReferencePoint Press, Inc.
Printed in the United States

For more information, contact:
ReferencePoint Press, Inc.
PO Box 27779
San Diego, CA 92198
www.ReferencePointPress.com

LIBRARY OF CONGRESS CATALOGING-IN-PUBLICATION DATA

Names: Mooney, Carla, 1970- author.
Title: What is the future of virtual reality? / by Carla Mooney.
Description: San Diego, CA : ReferencePoint Press, Inc, 2017. | Series: The future of technology series | Audience: Grades 9 to 12. | Includes bibliographical references and index.
Identifiers: LCCN 2016022845 (print) | LCCN 2016026308 (ebook) | ISBN 9781682820940 (hardback) | ISBN 9781682820957 (eBook)
Subjects: LCSH: Virtual reality--Juvenile literature. | Technological innovations--Juvenile literature.
Classification: LCC QA76.9.V5 M635 2017 (print) | LCC QA76.9.V5 (ebook) | DDC 006.8--dc23
LC record available at https://lccn.loc.gov/2016022845

Contents

Important Events in the Development of Virtual Reality

1957
Morton Heilig, considered the father of virtual reality, invents the Sensorama, a simulator with three-dimensional images to create the prototype of virtual reality.

1991
The Virtuality Group adds virtual reality to arcade video games.

1984
VPL Research, a developer of several virtual reality devices, is founded by virtual reality enthusiast Jaron Lanier.

1960   **1970**   **1980**   **1990**

1965
Computer scientist Ivan Sutherland comes up with the idea of using a head-mounted display connected to a computer to see a virtual world.

1987
The term *virtual reality* is first used by Jaron Lanier, founder of VPL Research.

1982
The movie *Tron* is the first film to depict characters entering a virtual world inside a computer.

1961
The Philco Corporation develops a helmet that includes a video screen and head-tracking system called Project Headsight.

1993
Sega introduces wraparound virtual reality glasses at the summer Consumer Electronics Show.

2016
Several new headsets, including the Oculus Rift, Sony's PlayStation VR, and HTC's Vive, are introduced to the public.

1997
Researchers at Georgia Tech use virtual reality to create war-zone scenarios to treat veterans with post-traumatic stress disorder.

2012
Palmer Luckey raises money on Kickstarter to fund the development of his Oculus Rift virtual reality headset.

1995   **2005**   **2015**

1995
Nintendo releases the Virtual Boy headset, which fails to attract consumers.

2014
Facebook purchases Oculus for nearly $2 billion; Google introduces its low-cost Google Cardboard virtual reality headset that operates with a smartphone.

1999
The movie *The Matrix* is released and features a computer-generated world.

2015
Samsung releases the Gear VR headset, the first modern-day virtual reality technology available for consumers.

Stepping Inside a New World

From Theory to Application

Virtual reality is a computer-generated simulation of a three-dimensional (3D) image or environment. A person using special electronic equipment, such as a head-mounted display or gloves with sensors, can interact with the images in a way that seems real. The 3D images change smoothly as the participant moves his or her head. To create a virtual reality environment, a computer sends video to a special head-mounted display or headset. The headset has two small screens, one in front of each eye, that display slightly different, stereoscopic images to create realistic 3D images of the virtual environment. Head-mounted displays also use position sensors to detect how a user is moving his or her head and body and then adjust the display accordingly. Users wear datagloves equipped with sensors to detect hand and finger motions or manipulate a wireless wand to touch, point, and interact within a virtual environment.

At the Surgery Brain Research Pavilion at the University of Chicago Medicine, first-year medical students put on 3D glasses and sit down in front of a video screen. As they look at the screen, the students manipulate a pen attached to a robotic arm that moves a virtual probe and pokes colored balls. The students are not playing a new video game. They are practicing basic tasks that are part of their med school training. Poking the colored balls to select the softest ones is similar to exploring the consistency of tissues in order to detect tumors. Neurosurgery residents are also using virtual reality to practice surgical procedures such as one that involves drilling a hole into a patient's skull to relieve pressure on the brain. Ben Roitberg, an associate professor of surgery, says the system has become an important part of training neurosurgeons at the university. "Residents do sets of certain procedures, or elements of procedures that require a high degree of coordination, spatial orientation and precision. Where there are many ways to be imprecise and dangerous, this kind of training is really helpful,"[1] he says.

The virtual reality system, which runs on a standard desktop computer, creates a visual simulation of a surgical procedure. It also provides haptic feedback, which gives users the sense of touch as they move the virtual surgical instruments. Roitberg says that the combination of the visual simulation on the screen with the haptic feedback from the robotic arm is important for learning delicate neurosurgical procedures. "I can do some surgeries with my eyes closed because it's all about touch. You have to imagine the anatomy," he says. "With this system you feel the resistance of the tissue and your position in space. You can even feel the vibration of the drill and how the bone gets removed."[2]

> **WORDS IN CONTEXT**
>
> **stereoscopic**
> The process by which two slightly different images of the same object are viewed together, which creates the illusion of depth.

In the past, medical students practiced procedures with plastic bones or cadavers. Then they assisted physicians with procedures on real patients. The virtual reality system creates another layer to medical training. The simulator provides feedback on how well the students perform their virtual procedures. It records success rates, how far a student was from his or her intended target, and whether the procedure was properly performed. The simulator can even track the vibration of the student's hand. According to Roitberg, this feedback is valuable for students because it can provide information about performance that a human observer cannot. Virtual reality systems can be used for any type of procedure that requires fine motor skills and involves delicate anatomy.

With virtual reality goggles, a user sees a computer-generated simulation of a 3D image. The brain is essentially tricked into thinking it sees reality rather than images and actions in a virtual world.

It can also help doctors prepare for rare, complicated procedures. "It is definitely a major future direction because ultimately, surgical simulation should be done fully in virtual reality," says Roitberg. "That's the way of the future, and that's how training and practice of any procedure can be repeated multiple times, cost-effectively, anywhere in the world."[3]

How It Works

People understand the world around them by using their sense and perception systems. Humans have five main senses: sight, hearing, taste, smell, and touch. Other sensory systems recognize temperature, pain, balance, vibration, and various other stimuli. All of these sensory systems send messages to the brain, which processes them. A person's entire experience of reality is a combination of all the sensory information received by the brain.

In virtual reality, a computer tricks the brain with a 3D, computer-generated environment. It takes what people expect to see in the real world and replaces it with images that move and behave in the same way. "Your perceptual system doesn't really have anything to tell it that it's not in the virtual world, so it believes it, and you feel as if you're present," says Mark Bolas, associate director of the Institute of Creative Technologies at the University of Southern California. When people watch a 3D movie, they see 3D images; however, when they turn their heads, they see the theater wall beyond the edges of the movie screen. Virtual reality uses computer graphics, algorithms, and lenses to change the picture as a person moves his or her head, effectively hiding the screen's edge and making it seem as if the screen never ends. If a person turns his or her head to the left or right, there is no edge to the screen as it surrounds the person 360 degrees. "All of a sudden, the trick's complete and you feel like you're in the space,"[4] says Bolas.

With a headset, a virtual reality system shows a person an image. When the person moves his or her head, the computer changes the image to make it seem as if the person is really there. The person becomes part of the virtual world and is able to manipulate objects or perform a series of actions. An effective virtual reality experience causes users to become unaware of their actual environment and focus on their presence in the virtual world.

Most virtual reality systems use computers that run software necessary to create virtual environments. Powerful graphics cards, originally designed for video gaming, are used in virtual environments. Headsets display images to users on two high-resolution liquid crystal display (LCD) screens— one for each eye. Separating the image into two parts is called stereoscopy, and it tricks the brain into creating a perception of depth and thinking it is in a fully 3D world.

Many Potential Applications

Although virtual reality is best known for its applications in gaming, the technology has many other potential applications—in medicine, entertainment, education, business, and the military. It has the potential to become a powerful tool for surgical training, product design, employee and soldier training, and engaging students. According to a report by MarketsandMarkets, a market research firm, the virtual reality market is expected to grow to $407.51 million with more than 25 million users by 2018. Mark Zuckerberg, chief executive officer (CEO) of Facebook, believes that virtual reality will be the next technology to change the world, predicting that it will become a major computing and communication platform in the future. "One day, we believe this kind of immersive, augmented reality will become a part of daily life for billions of people,"[5] says Zuckerberg.

Chapter 1

Immersive Entertainment

At a 1965 meeting of international computer experts, computer graphics pioneer Ivan Sutherland spoke about the possibility of using a computer to create a virtual world. At the time, the term *virtual reality* was not yet in use, but that is exactly what Sutherland was describing when he said this world would contain "a room within which the computer can control the existence of matter. A chair displayed in such a room would be good enough to sit in. Handcuffs displayed in such a room would be confining, and a bullet displayed in such a room would be fatal. With appropriate programming, such a display could literally be the Wonderland into which Alice walked."[6]

As the technology needed to create virtual reality has advanced rapidly in recent years, Sutherland's vision seems to be moving closer to reality. The gaming industry is leading the push for this technology, envisioning a virtual world where a gamer can experience being in a 3D environment and interacting with it as part of a game.

Early Attempts

During the 1990s several companies attempted to create virtual reality headsets for gaming. Nintendo released the Virtual Boy headset in 1995, promising true 3D graphics in gaming for the first time. However, the headset was clunky and gave users bad headaches. As a result, the Virtual Boy failed to catch on; within a year Nintendo had abandoned it. A string of other headset failures nearly extinguished interest in virtual reality technology. At the time, technology was not sophisticated enough to deliver a true immersive environment. Video screens did not have high enough resolution and were not able to refresh quickly enough to display a smooth image. And computer processors were not powerful enough to use a sufficient number of pixels in the images to create a convincing virtual world. These attempts at virtual reality headsets failed so completely that the entire field of virtual reality was pushed aside for more than a decade.

But all of that changed in 2012, when twenty-year-old Palmer Luckey launched a Kickstarter campaign that raised $2.5 million to develop the prototype of his Oculus Rift virtual reality headset. By this time, technology had started to catch up with the idea of virtual reality. The technology developed for smartphones, such as high-resolution screens, accurate motion sensors, and compact components, could be used for virtual reality headsets. Interest in virtual reality soared again.

The search engine giant Google joined the race to develop virtual reality in 2015 when it demonstrated how smartphones could be used for a basic virtual reality headset. Google introduced the Google Cardboard, a simple headset actually made of cardboard that holds a compatible smartphone in place. After downloading a virtual reality app to the phone, a user can strap on the cardboard headset and enjoy several virtual reality experiences. A version of Google Earth's 3D map program allows users to fly over cities or mountain ranges. Other apps take users climbing in Yosemite, speeding on roller coasters, scaring them with short horror movies, or taking them onstage with Paul McCartney. "Virtual reality will have an important role to play in entertainment, communications, work, and learning," says Clay Bavor, who leads Google's virtual reality project. "We've seen the proof that you can create wonderful virtual reality experiences with today's smartphone hardware; the sensors and the hardware and the content are only going to get better."[7]

Stepping into the Game

By 2016 Luckey's Oculus Rift, HTC's Vive, and Sony's PlayStation VR were showing the world where the future of virtual reality is headed. With any of these headsets, users see 3D images in all

The search engine giant Google has introduced Cardboard (pictured), a relatively simple virtual reality headset made from cardboard. When paired with a smartphone and app, Cardboard enables users to fly over cities, climb mountains, and more.

directions and feel as though they are part of the scene. According to technology news website CNET senior editor Jeff Bakalar, Oculus Rift is a promising virtual reality headset with the potential to get even better over time. He points out that although Oculus can currently only detect a user's head movement, with the introduction of Oculus Touch controllers, users will be able to make hand gestures and reach into virtual space. "For me, the most compelling thing about virtual reality isn't necessarily where it's at right now, but the notion of what is possible in the future five to 10 years down the road," says Bakalar. "We know the tech's limitations right now—viewing angle, resolution, bulkiness—but we see a future where all of those shortcomings are addressed in more comfortable gear, higher-res images, and even the idea that the

Music

The newest way to enjoy a concert may soon be inside a headset worn in the comfort of one's own home. The virtual reality company NextVR plans to release Coldplay's *Ghost Stories* concert tour in virtual reality. A clip of the first song, "A Sky Full of Stars," is available on the NextVR app and can be watched with a Samsung Gear virtual reality headset. The virtual reality concert puts fans onstage with the band members.

Two other companies, iHeartRadio and Universal Media Group, announced that they were partnering to bring music lovers virtually into the heart of several concerts in 2016. They plan to create immersive live music virtual reality experiences that can be enjoyed by large numbers of people across the country. The virtual reality experiences will vary by concert and by artist. Some will be of preshow, following the artist as he or she prepares for a concert, and other experiences will take place during or after a concert. These experiences can give music lovers a more personal viewing experience, with 360-degree views and virtual interactions with the artists and audience.

image could be projected right onto your retina, instead of looking through a lens at a small screen."[8]

The Rift headset is mainly intended for gaming, with available games such as *EVE: Valkyrie* and *Job Simulator: The 2050 Archives* specially designed to work with the virtual reality headset and give users an immersive gaming experience. Alex Hern, a technology reporter for the British newspaper the *Guardian*, was able to test the final prerelease version of Rift in late December 2015. He put on the headset and sat down to play *EVE: Valkyrie*, a game that puts players into the cockpit of a star fighter to battle various spacecraft in zero gravity. It is a fast-paced dogfight that is interactive and immersive. Hern described the experience, saying,

> I finally saw what the fuss was about. Wearing the device . . . I sat in a spaceship, gazing around at the cavernous hanger within which it sat. A string of lights turned on in front of my ship, which began accelerating faster and faster until, suddenly, it emerged from the side of an enormous

capital ship (which I could see if I craned my neck behind me), and I was left floating in the calmness of space. That was when the enemies ported in.[9]

Some of the world's top video game makers are working to develop more virtual reality games for devices like Oculus Rift and PlayStation VR. Brian Blau, an analyst with the information technology and research company Gartner, cautions that the success of virtual reality gaming will depend on the content being developed:

The virtual reality experience is completely dependent on the device and the quality of the content. I'm convinced that the initial devices being released in 2016 are good enough, but it's the content that must keep users coming back. Is there enough good virtual reality content in the pipeline to keep users engaged with the devices over time? From early indications there are some great virtual reality games and video experiences so I'm not worried, but ultimately this is a question that we can't answer until we see how the general public reacts to these new types of personal computing devices and content.[10]

One potential barrier to widespread use of virtual reality for gaming is cost. In addition to the cost of the headset, virtual reality games can only run on powerful—and costly—computers. The high price of the headsets and the accompanying technology may discourage some people from purchasing the devices. Luckey believes that this barrier is only temporary and that the computer technology needed to run his Oculus Rift will be available to the mainstream public at an affordable price within a few years. "Most people don't have computers with high-end graphics cards. In the future, that's going to change: give it five or six years, and most computers will be capable of running good virtual experiences,"[11] he said in December 2015.

Facebook founder Mark Zuckerberg was so impressed with the potential of Oculus Rift that he bought it for $2 billion in 2014. With Facebook's funding, a team of virtual reality experts led by

Luckey are working to further refine and improve Oculus Rift's virtual reality experience. The team is working on incorporating more senses, including technologies that capture scent and touch. Zuckerberg sees a limitless future for the virtual reality technology that Oculus Rift is based on. "This is just the start. After games, we're going to make Oculus a platform for many other experiences," he writes. "Imagine enjoying a court side seat at a game, studying in a classroom of students and teachers all over the world or consulting with a doctor face-to-face—just by putting on goggles in your home."[12]

Films: Larger than Life

Already several nongaming uses for virtual reality technology in entertainment have emerged. Movie studios have embraced virtual reality as a way to give moviegoers a new way to experience film. Twentieth Century Fox, Lionsgate, Disney, Marvel, and Warner Brothers have all released special virtual reality videos. In 2015 Twentieth Century Fox announced a partnership with Oculus to bring more than one hundred movies to Oculus Video, a new virtual reality video app. The films include box-office hits and Oscar-winning titles such as *Birdman*, *Alien*, *Die Hard*, and *Cast Away*. "VR cinema is a new way of presenting our movies, and has the opportunity to bring in mass market consumers to virtual reality," says Mike Dunn, president of Twentieth Century Fox Home Entertainment. "With Oculus Video, we are leveraging the scale and flexibility of mobile devices, while continuing to deliver a powerful, emotional experience for consumers. We are just scratching the surface of how Hollywood and virtual reality will revolutionize entertainment by exploring innovative ways to develop immersive experiences as a new storytelling medium,"[13] says Dunn.

With virtual reality, film studios can share new experiences with audiences and let them experience stories as if they are part of the action. In January 2016 Twentieth Century Fox came out with a demo version of *The Martian VR Experience*, a companion to the 2015 feature film titled *The Martian* starring Matt Damon as an astronaut stranded on Mars. In this thirty-minute virtual reality experience, director Robert Stromberg created several interactive

In the 2015 movie The Martian, *Matt Damon's character struggles to survive after being left behind on Mars. A companion virtual reality piece allows viewers to share in some of the character's experiences.*

segments that mirror the actions of Damon's character, Mark Watney, as he tries to survive alone on Mars. Using an Oculus Touch controller, the experience lets viewers throw potatoes into buckets, navigate cold space, drive a rover, and salvage solar panels just as Damon's character did in the movie. "One of the things that's so intriguing about this medium is creating the illusion that something's actually happening to you," says Ted Schilowitz, a director at the Fox Innovation Lab. "Am I believing this is actually happening to me? I'm no longer watching a movie or television show; this is actually happening around me."[14] Fox planned to release *The Martian VR Experience* to Rift, Vive, and Gear users by the end of 2016.

Virtual reality in movies was also on display during the 2016 Sundance Film Festival New Frontier program, which highlights new or alternative forms of creative expression. One project, called *The Climb*, was made by 8i, a start-up company that creates virtual reality content. The project puts viewers on the edge of a cliff hundreds of feet above a river. Then a voice tells the viewer to jump. "Your logical side is saying, 'I'm in a headset. I'm in this room.' But your emotional side is saying, 'I'm on a cliff. I could die here. I don't want to jump,'"[15] says 8i cofounder and CEO Linc Gasking. According to 8i executive creative director Rainer Gombos, virtual reality expands the possibilities of storytelling. "You can immerse the viewer into worlds—artificial or reality-like worlds—that you couldn't do before," he says. "You can move around in the scene and look around at things from different angles. You can tell stories. You can entertain. You can have people experience larger-than-life events."[16]

Documentaries: Building Empathy

Several filmmakers have been experimenting with using virtual reality in documentaries. By bringing the viewer into the story, filmmakers hope to create more empathy in their audiences. Freelance videographer Christian Stephen's film *Welcome to Aleppo* uses virtual reality technology to let viewers experience the effects of the Syrian civil war. Working with production company RYOT and Syrian journalist Adnan Hadad, Stephen's film puts viewers in the middle of Aleppo's bombed-out buildings and quiet streets. "VR is the most exciting technology we've found. It puts people squarely in the shoes of somebody else, so they can see through their eyes and experience the scale of devastation in some of these places. Scale is a really important aspect to this," says producer Bryn Mooser, who is also cofounder of RYOT. "When you're in these places in real life, you're seeing the scale: the scope of the disaster and how big a crisis [it] is. That's something that's very difficult to translate through traditional photography, or even through film. Virtual reality is going to change disaster and crisis-response filmmaking for good."[17]

WORDS IN CONTEXT

empathy
The ability to understand and share the feelings of another person.

Filmmaker Chris Milk has also worked on several short virtual reality documentaries, including *Clouds over Sidra*, a film about a refugee camp in Jordan, and *Waves of Grace*, the story of an Ebola

Unwelcome Side Effects

For some people, virtual reality can lead to a not-so-pleasant reality: nausea and vertigo. Virtual reality headsets, along with 3D movies, can cause virtual reality sickness. Similar to traditional motion sickness, symptoms of virtual reality sickness include headache, nausea, vomiting, pallor, sweating, fatigue, drowsiness, and disorientation. The effects vary by person and usually depend on the type of game or movie and the length of time the person spends wearing a headset. "After a morning's worth of different Rift games, I felt disorientated, a touch nauseous and distinctly headachey," wrote user Keza MacDonald. "After five hours, I felt like I needed a lie-down in a dark room."

Developers are working to figure out what causes the virtual reality sickness and correct it. Most believe that the main problem arises when on-screen graphics do not keep up with a user's head movements. In addition, a sensory disconnect could trigger virtual sickness, such as when visual cues from the virtual world tell users that they are walking, but body cues tell them that they are sitting down. Potential fixes include making sure that the frame rate is fast enough not to trigger nausea. Creating sounds that match the virtual environment may also help because it helps to orient the user in the virtual world.

Quoted in Derrik J. Lang, "For Virtual Reality Creators, Motion Sickness a Real Issue," Phys.org, March 18, 2016. http://phys.org.

survivor in Liberia. Milk hopes that his films and those made by others will help people realize that virtual reality can be used for more than just gaming—it can be a powerful storytelling tool. "Being able to put people in the place gives them not just a better sense of it, but gives them more empathy and a deeper emotional connection to the people that were actually there," says Milk. "That's where the true power of virtual reality lies in regards to journalism."[18]

Television: In the Middle of the Action

Television is yet another medium that may experience significant changes as virtual reality technology develops. Oculus founder Luckey has gone so far as to declare that virtual reality headsets will eventually replace televisions because they are cheaper, better for the environment, and offer a more dynamic viewing experience. Some in the industry were skeptical of Luckey's comments. They recalled statements made by others in 2009 about the bright future of 3D television. Years later, 3D television still has not taken off with the public. Executives at several cable and network television companies are not taking any chances, however. They have begun investing heavily in virtual reality technology, betting that it is the future of entertainment. Disney has spent $66 million funding Jaunt, a virtual reality start-up. And media outlets such as ABC News and National Geographic have rented Immersive Media's 360-degree cameras for new virtual reality programming and advertisements.

Comcast and Time Warner have also poured millions of dollars into a new venture called NextVR. Virtual reality has the potential to put sports fans right in the middle of the action. It can give viewers the ability to sit courtside at a National Basketball Association (NBA) game or have a 360-degree view of the action at a soccer match. The NBA made its first foray into this new technology when it broadcast a live game in virtual reality in 2015. NextVR and Turner Sports live-streamed the league's opening night tip-off between the Golden State Warriors and the New Orleans Pelicans. Fans who owned a Samsung Gear virtual reality headset could access the live stream via NextVR on the Oculus app.

NextVR has already signed a five-year deal with Fox Sports to do live virtual reality broadcasts of professional sporting events. "It's important for us to be at the forefront of how sports fans are consuming content well into the future. I think virtual reality represents that," says David Nathanson, head of business operations for Fox Sports. "We believe what NextVR is doing in live sports is best in class."[19] Under this partnership, NextVR and Fox Sports offered fans a virtual reality experience of the 2016 Daytona 500. NextVR's cameras followed the action around the track while viewers watched on an Android device through an Oculus virtual reality headset. Viewers saw a combination of a

If 3D television had succeeded, it is possible it would have looked something like this. But the bright future once seen for 3D TV has faded and left some experts skeptical about where virtual reality might be headed.

live feed from three cameras and prerecorded content. "Just as you would guide the direction of a broadcast show, we guide the audience for the best view for whatever is going on and then lay in some graphics," says Matt Amick, postproduction supervisor at NextVR. "We mimic what it's like to be here, but we're also enhancing that experience."[20]

Michael Davies, a senior vice president of field and technical operations at Fox Sports, says that Fox's production of live sporting events will continue to evolve as virtual reality technology improves. "When [virtual reality] becomes a regular part of the viewer experience depends a lot on how the consumer devices develop and how good they wind up becoming," he says. "These devices are good but have a long way to go. But we have also come a long way in the last year. Auto racing is one of those things where we can put the viewer in places they never would have been able to go."[21]

The Future of Virtual Reality Entertainment

Virtual reality's ability to create immersive and engaging entertainment—whether in gaming or documentaries or sporting events—suggests all sorts of future potential. Several companies are hoping to add new dimensions to virtual reality, such as making it a full-body experience with seating that moves and shakes along with a movie or television show. As companies create more content and prices of headsets and related technology decrease, the demand for virtual reality technology is expected to grow. "Just look at any house with an Xbox or Wii. It's going to be that common," says Stromberg. "Every house will have a VR headset. Every house will give a person the option to sort of escape for a minute, or to play a game, or to look up what it's like to go to this hotel . . . on vacation or whatever. As we all have laptop computers to find things, there will be a new way to tell for sure if you want to experience something. There'll be a new way to escape or entertain."[22]

Chapter 2

Engaging Education

In March 2016, students at Watertown Middle School visited Greece, Iceland, and various World War II sites—all without leaving their Massachusetts school. Instead of hopping on a plane, students strapped on Google Cardboard virtual reality headsets equipped with smartphones and took a virtual tour. The school librarian introduced the technology to students, explaining that they were being given the opportunity to test the Google Expeditions application, a virtual reality platform built for the classroom. Using a master tablet to control the scenes being viewed, the teachers led their eighth-grade students through sites related to World War II. First they visited Pearl Harbor in Hawaii, which was bombed by Japanese aircraft in 1941. Next they visited the Auschwitz-Birkenau memorial and museum in Poland, where they explored the concentration camp in which hundreds of thousands of Jews and others were subjected to horrendous treatment or killed. As part of the lesson, their teachers pointed out the buildings that once served as prisoner barracks. Sites like these had been described by Elie Wiesel in his book *Night*, which the class was reading as part of a unit on the Holocaust. "In addition to students trying it, teachers are trying it out to see if they could use it in their curriculum, if it's a worthy investment,"[23] school librarian Leah Maroni-Wagner says.

Students already use technology such as tablets, smartphones, and netbooks in the classroom. They use technology to share text, record and watch videos, and research topics. Virtual reality, which would allow students to experience immersive, 360-degree environments, is poised to be the next frontier for technology in the classroom. Numerous companies have emerged to provide schools with curriculum, content, teacher training, and technology tools to support virtual reality learning in schools. "I think once teachers have tried virtual reality with their classes, they will realize it opens up their students' imaginations to the world beyond their textbooks, Chromebooks and tablets,"[24] says an investor in one of these companies.

Field Trips Across the World

Virtual reality has the potential to take students on virtual field trips all over the world. Google executives recognized this potential when they launched the Expeditions virtual reality classroom application in 2015. The idea for Expeditions came from an employee challenge to create a tool to better engage students. Jennifer Holland, now the Expeditions product manager, says that they combined existing Google products—Cardboard, some teaching apps, and an archive of 3D maps and photographs. Combining all of them led to the project's interactive virtual reality experiences. "It's a really practical application of virtual reality and a way to use cutting edge tech for schools," says Holland. "We're not just taking old tech and throwing it over the fence. We thought a lot about how this would be helpful."[25]

Google engineers worked with teachers and content partners around the world to create more than one hundred virtual journeys. On these trips, students can experience the world in locations as varied as the ancient ruins at Machu Picchu to the ice sheets of remote Antarctica. One virtual journey allows students to dive underwater and explore Australia's Great Barrier Reef. Another takes students on a visit to Buckingham Palace, the official London residence and administrative headquarters of reigning British monarchs dating back centuries.

Although some of the content is two-dimensional (2D), newer journeys feature 3D video shot from Google's Jump camera rig, which holds sixteen GoPro cameras at one time. Google takes the video shot by all sixteen cameras and puts it together into a lifelike 3D video. The technology will allow an English teacher to take students to Italy to view the setting for Shakespeare's *Romeo and Juliet* or a social

Second-grade students in North Carolina experience virtual reality panoramas with Google Expeditions. Using Expeditions, students can travel far and wide and even to different time periods in history.

studies teacher to bring a class to the Great Wall of China. "I was in a ninth grade classroom recently and watched as the kids were able to really compare the architecture of the Duomo in Florence and the Pantheon in Rome," says Expeditions program manager Holland. "The teacher had come prepared to talk about this with some black and white photos she had printed out. But to see the kids really come to life when they felt like they were in these places was amazing."[26]

Virtual Classrooms

Beyond elementary schools, virtual reality is also coming to college classrooms. At Harvard Business School, students engage in a lively discussion with business administration professor Bharat Anand about whether ride-share company Uber is worth $50 billion. Yet there are no students in Anand's classroom. Instead,

Virtually Unwrap a Mummy

At the Museum of Mediterranean and Near Eastern Antiquities in Stockholm, Sweden, visitors can use virtual reality to "unwrap" a mummy. The museum staff digitally scanned several mummies using a computed tomography scanner. Then they used the scans and some 2D pictures of the sarcophagi and mummies taken from different angles to create a 3D model. The museum has turned this work into a virtual exhibit for visitors. Visitors can use a giant touch screen on a digital autopsy table to digitally unwrap one of the mummies, believed to be an ancient Egyptian priest. Starting with the sarcophagus, visitors peel away layers of the coffin, down to the mummy's remains. With each layer, visitors use their hands to zoom in and out and rotate the 3D model. "The technology will enable our visitors to gain a deeper understanding of the men and women inside the mummy wrappings," says Elna Nord, producer of the exhibition. "Layer by layer, the visitor can unwrap the mummy and gain knowledge of the individual's sex, age, living conditions and beliefs. With help from the technology, the mummies become so much stronger mediators of knowledge of our past."

Quoted in BBC News, "Museum Visitors Can 'Unwrap' a Mummy," June 28, 2013. www.bbc.com.

he is teaching in a virtual classroom located in the local public broadcasting company's offices. His sixty students are scattered around the world. In this virtual classroom, Anand lectures in a broadcast studio while a camerawoman follows him with a camera on her shoulder. Five stationary cameras also film, and a director puts the multiple images together into one feed, like a live television show. Another person makes sure that the live audio from the students is loud and clear, as if they were present in the classroom. A high-resolution video wall shows images of the sixty students. Whether they are in London or San Francisco, the students feel as if they are sitting front and center in the class.

Although setting up a virtual classroom takes more planning and behind-the-scenes effort than a professor walking into a traditional classroom to give a lecture, Anand says that the extra work is worth it. "You walk in here and there is just this energy," he says. "You can see someone who is up at 3 a.m. in the Philippines, someone in Seattle and another in Mumbai. This feels like you are literally in the classroom, and the feedback we're getting is that this is every bit as engaging as being in the classroom—but more intense."[27] Anand's students agree. "I couldn't take my eyes off the screen," says Dave Schroeder, one of the students in the virtual class. "It felt like everyone was in the same room."[28]

In addition to classes, Harvard uses its virtual classroom for research seminars and sessions for master of business administration (MBA) students who are traveling abroad on school trips. In the future, Harvard could offer a global executive MBA program that is entirely virtual.

Enhancing STEM Education

Virtual reality can be used to make complex subjects come to life. STEM (science, technology, engineering, and math) education is one of the hottest areas of study around the world. Careers in STEM fields are in demand. According to the Bureau of Labor Statistics, employment in STEM jobs is projected to grow to more than 9 million between 2012 and 2022, an increase of about 1 million jobs. To prepare students for these opportunities, educators, industry leaders, and others have encouraged an increase in STEM courses in high school and college. Yet studies have found that as many as half of students who take STEM courses in college end up changing their major. Many complain that traditional STEM education, with lectures and the occasional lab, is too heavily focused on abstract theories and does not give students many opportunities to experience STEM firsthand.

Virtual reality technology can make it possible for students to experience STEM concepts in a hands-on, interactive, and immersive way. It can be used to help students see practical applications for theories and technology. Complex and tedious content could be presented to students in more exciting ways. High school students in Indiana, for example, were able to apply engineering concepts in a project that involved building virtual reality racetracks. This project was sponsored by La Plaza, an educational nonprofit in Indiana, and staff from the Advanced Visualization Laboratory at Indiana University.

In this artist's conception, a fearsome tyrannosaurus chases a velociraptor. Google Cardboard has an app that transports students all the way back to the time of the dinosaurs.

Other applications are also being developed and tested. Google Cardboard has an app called VR Jurassic Land, which transports students back to a time when dinosaurs roamed the earth. In Chemistry VR, students explore chemistry topics from their own homes in a simulated lab. Developers from Florida State University (FSU) are also working on a new app called Earthquake Rebuild, which uses architecture to teach geometry and other math skills. In Earthquake Rebuild, students are fully immersed in a 3D town after an earthquake. They apply math, engineering, and science technologies to rebuild the town. When rebuilding, students consider architectural principles like symmetry and balance while also making artistic choices about color. In addition, students have to budget their virtual finances for the rebuilding project. "A lot of kids don't realize math is everywhere. Architecture can encourage them to think about what math is. It's not just formulas," says Fengfeng Ke, an assistant professor at FSU and the app's lead developer. Ke says that the app targets middle school students because they are at a critical age for learning and developing a passion for math.

In Europe, the Formula Student Competition is exciting and engaging STEM students. The Institution of Mechanical Engineers runs this educational motorsport competition. Engineering students across Europe design and build a single-seat racing car to compete in a variety of events. At the University of Liverpool in England, teams used virtual reality technology from Virtalis, a company based in the United Kingdom, to design their cars. The technology allowed each student to virtually design a car; then, as a team, they decided which design was the best. "The visualization really helps get the students involved, and we'll hear them say, 'WOW I never thought I'd get to do this. I'm so pleased I took this course,'"[29] says Andrew Connell, Virtalis's chief technology officer. Connell believes that a new generation of students will be more excited about STEM careers with virtual reality as one of the teaching tools.

Training Teachers

Students are not the only ones who will benefit from virtual reality in the classroom. Virtual reality technology is also being used to train student teachers. One of the biggest hurdles to becoming a successful teacher is knowing how to manage the behavior of a class full of students. A new virtual reality simulator, TeachLiVE, is helping student teachers hone the skills they will need in front of a real class. In use at more than eighty-five schools across the United States, the TeachLiVE simulator puts prospective teachers in front of five avatar students and gives the teachers instant feedback on their performance. "Classroom management is the single biggest challenge faced by every beginning teacher, and the most frequent area they and their principals mention for needing additional training," says Robert Pianta, dean of the Curry School of Education at the University of Virginia. "To be able to start teaching on day one with more proficiency in classroom management and more confidence in your management skills could not be more valuable to a beginning teacher and the students with whom they work."[30]

At the Curry School of Education, student teachers are using the TeachLiVE virtual reality simulator. To begin each ten-minute training session, student teachers stand in front of a video monitor in a small studio. A faculty supervisor begins the simulation, and the five avatar students come to life. While the student teacher goes through his or her lesson, the avatar students go through a variety of behaviors to which the student teacher responds. They might pull out a cell phone to send a text or make an unkind comment to another student. If the virtual students become disruptive, the student teacher can practice strategies he or she has learned to manage and refocus their behavior. The faculty supervisor controls the virtual students' responses to the student teacher's actions. While it does not replace real-world student teaching experience, the virtual reality program gives student teachers a place to test strategies, make mistakes, and learn from them. "It's a guided practice environment," says Catherine Bradshaw, a professor at the Curry School of Education. "The simulator provides an opportunity for students to get guided practice and on-the-spot feedback on their use of different strategies used in the classroom."[31]

Bradshaw says that although it might seem strange at first, the virtual classroom is a good place for students to improve their skills before they get in front of live students. For the first few minutes, the student teachers might feel self-conscious interacting with a computer screen, but the lifelike avatars quickly make the interactions seem real. "What we want to do is help teachers practice these strategies so that they can use them more flexibly in a real-world setting,"[32] says Bradshaw.

WORDS IN CONTEXT

avatar
An icon or figure representing a person in a computer game or simulation.

Head-Mounted Display

To enter most virtual reality environments, users put on a head-mounted display (HMD). An HMD is a computer display that the user wears on his or her head. An HMD can be mounted in a pair of goggles or a helmet. No matter where the user looks, the HMD monitor stays in front of the user's eyes. An HMD includes a device that tracks the position and movement of a user's head so that the computer knows where the user is looking.

To display images, most HMD's have two screens—one for each eye—which gives the perception of depth. In an HMD, most display monitors are LCDs. LCD monitors are smaller, more lightweight, and more efficient than older cathode-ray tube (CRT) displays. Many HMDs include speakers or headphones that provide sound to enhance the virtual reality experience. HMDs are typically tethered to a computer by one or more cables. To date, wireless connections are too slow to refresh the images quickly enough.

Pianta believes that the virtual reality simulator can be used in areas beyond the teacher education program to train other professions that work with youth. "This use of the . . . simulator in our teacher preparation program is, I hope, just the beginning of our developing a very robust and deep capacity to use simulation in our professional preparation programs," he says. "Clearly this type of experience is of great value in preparing teachers, but we also see its value in preparation across a number of professional roles—for example, in school counseling, psychology, educational leadership and in the broader area of working with youth."[33]

Museum Exhibits and Tours

Museums are also using virtual reality technology to educate and immerse visitors. At the Salvador Dali Museum in St. Petersburg, Florida, a new virtual reality exhibit is taking art appreciation to a new level. Museum visitors can use virtual reality to step inside one of Salvador Dali's paintings. In the *Dreams of Dali* exhibit, visitors put on Oculus Rift headsets and enter Dali's *Archeological Reminiscence of Millet's "Angelus"* painting. They can move

A museum visitor views a beautifully decorated sarcophagus from ancient Egypt. Continued advances in virtual reality technology might make it possible for virtual visitors to tour museum exhibits from anywhere in the world.

around and explore elements in the painting as well as recurring motifs from some of Dali's other paintings. "You actually have a three-dimensional feeling that you're inside a painting. . . . It's actually like there are objects closer and further away and you're walking amidst them. It's a vulnerable feeling you give yourself up to. It's not like anything you've ever felt before,"[34] says Jeff Goodby, a spokesperson for Goodby Silverstein & Partners, the firm that created the virtual reality experience. Although the creative team started with Dali's painting, it also tried to give visitors a look into Dali's imagination. "It required a lot of research both from a technological standpoint and on Dali himself," says Sam Luchini, creative director at Goodby Silverstein & Partners. "How do the figures look from the back? Luckily Dali recreated many of the elements in other works so we were able to accurately reflect them in our virtual reality experience. Technology-wise, we wanted to create a world people were free to explore as they wished and, ultimately, provided with a more engaged way to experience art."[35]

Other museums have created hands-on exhibits that allow visitors to use virtual reality to explore ancient artifacts. At the British Museum, visitors in August 2015 were transported to the Bronze Age. Using Samsung Gear virtual reality headsets, museum visitors were able to walk inside a four-thousand-year-old roundhouse, where they found a flickering fire and changing levels of light shining through an open door. They were also able to explore several items from the museum's collection that had been scanned in 3D and placed in the virtual reality landscape. "The technology is particularly useful for the bronze age, a difficult period for visitors to engage with and imagine museum objects in their original context,"[36] says Neil Wilkin, a curator at the museum.

The Future of Learning

The application of virtual reality to enhance education is in the earliest stages. As technology improves and more content is created, virtual reality has the potential to revolutionize how people around the world learn. Museum curators could lead thousands of virtual visitors through an exhibit. Professors could teach virtual classes to students around the world. In addition, it may one day be possible for elementary school students from the United States to participate in a virtual field trip with peers from another country. "360-degree immersive VR [virtual reality], especially in a classroom setting, will revolutionize education methodology," says Brandon Farwell, an investor in the virtual reality company Nearpod. "Students can affordably be transported to a novel 360-degree medium, whether it's touring the Smithsonian or learning about the hard sciences like astronomy or anatomy. By using an affordable headset . . . and a smartphone, teachers enable students to unlock their imaginations and enjoy learning."[37]

Chapter 3

Virtual Reality in Business

At the Sundance Film Festival in January 2016, outdoor foot-wear company Merrell debuted TrailScape, the company's first virtual reality experience for consumers. Created by visual effects company Framestore, TrailScape allows users to take a virtual walk through the Dolomite Mountains in Italy. In addition to the virtual reality immersion, the experience includes real objects such as ropes to mark a bridge, a rock wall, and fans to simulate wind. Users put on an Oculus Rift headset and feel like they are walking over a wooden bridge and ledge high in the mountains. TrailScape's launch coincides with the release of Merrell's latest Capra hiking boot. According to company president Gene McCarthy, Merrell decided to invest in virtual reality and digital technology to reach a broader consumer base. "I wanted to freshen the brand up and give it a loud voice, but I wanted to do it in a way that was appealing to a broader audience and that's more youthful,"[38] says McCarthy. Jamie Mandor, Merrell's head of global brand marketing, says that technology is the best way to reach the company's target market—outdoor enthusiasts seeking adventure. "It's changing the way we speak and communicate with our customers," says Mandor. "Taking that first step into virtual was a great way to inspire those adventures."[39]

Development of TrailScape took about six months. Mandor had originally wanted users to be able to see their shoes to highlight Merrell products. That proved to be impossible when designers realized that Oculus Rift currently does not have the capability for users to see their own body while immersed in TrailScape. "It's a brave new world in a lot of ways," says Mike Woods, executive creative director at Framestore. "It's highly unlikely that the original concept will be the final deliverable [product] because we learn stuff as we go."[40]

Excitement is building as virtual reality is poised to transform how businesses operate. Many companies are investing in research and development so that they can decide how to best use this technology to improve their business and better satisfy customers.

Product Design and Engineering

Engineers are already using virtual reality systems to design and create virtual products that can be used to test design principles, safety, and more, without the expense and time involved in building a physical prototype. When engineers at the defense and security company BAE Systems are developing a new, state-of-the-art submarine, they no longer use scale models. Instead, they put on virtual reality headsets to manipulate 3D virtual models. This approach allows them to find design flaws earlier and prevent them from becoming expensive corrections down the road. "People can walk around a scale model and interact with it," says Sarah Cockburn-Price, spokesperson for the virtual reality company Virtalis, which is working with BAE's engineers. "It breaks down barriers because the team can share and work on it from different locations, and work out how to best manufacture it."[41]

Virtual reality can benefit product design and development teams by enhancing their understanding of a new product and ways to improve its performance. "We kind of trap engineers behind the computer screen now, so they can only touch a product with a mouse," says Andrew Connell of Virtalis. "But we want people to become immersed in their 3D model; to reach in with their hands and really dig about inside a product to explore, learn about, and improve it, while also communicating with others in the organization about that product." Using Virtalis's Visionary Render VR software, engineers, marketers, project managers, and others can virtually collaborate on new products. "The VR systems network

Design teams can enhance their understanding of new product performance by using 3D models and virtual reality. This technology makes it easier for team members at various locations to work collaboratively.

people together so they all see the same product on their screens and can have a meeting around this product," Connell says. "So if somebody in, say Bristol, moves a component, everyone else sees it move."[42]

For heavy equipment manufacturer Caterpillar, virtual reality saves time in the product design phase. Caterpillar's virtual reality system puts designers in front of a large screen with 3D glasses. The system uses special glasses and a camera to track a user's motion. Designers move a remote similar to a Nintendo Wii remote to navigate 3D models of the product they are working on. Designers can virtually walk around the scale model, climb on it, and duck below parts of it. Designers can also slice the machine in half to inspect its inner workings. "This allows us to understand customer interactions early to inform the proper design," says Galen Faidley of Caterpillar. Beyond that, virtual reality makes it possible for designers to spot design flaws, make adjustments, and create assembly instructions before the product even reaches the manufacturing floor. "We're able to validate and price out our design before it hits the factory. In the past you'd throw it over the wall to the factory and they would have to figure out the sequence it would be assembled in."[43] Representatives from the factory come into the virtual reality lab and also examine the virtual machine and make recommendations on any changes or adjustments to the design. Using virtual reality allows designers to make changes fairly late in the development process, without causing a problem in manufacturing.

Virtual Training for Workers

With virtual reality, employers can safely test their workers in a range of environments and scenarios. "If you're training to work on an oil rig, it's much safer to have that experience in the virtual world rather than the North Sea, as well as saving you time and materials,"[44] says Jason Collins, marketing director of visualization specialists ZeroLight. In addition, training employees with video games and virtual reality experiences creates a hands-on approach that is more efficient and engaging. "We learn by experiencing," says Erin Marietta, chief operating officer at Louisiana Immersive Technologies Enterprise (LITE), a company that creates virtual reality gaming software. "Everyone learns in an environment where you can touch and feel. And that's what virtual reality does. It's getting cheaper and a lot easier to produce."[45]

Several oil companies have embraced virtual reality as a way to train their workers. Instead of attending classes and watching PowerPoint presentations, workers play custom video games that teach them safety, rules, and procedures on an oil rig. Ultimately, the virtual training could save lives. According to the Bureau of Labor Statistics, the fatality rate in the oil and gas extraction industry is about eight times higher than the average fatality rate for all other US industries. Training in a virtual environment can give oil workers the experience they need to work offshore safely. "When you have workers who have never been on an offshore platform, they don't know what to expect,"

> **WORDS IN CONTEXT**
>
> **scale model**
> A smaller physical representation of an object, with the same characteristics and proportions.

says Skyra Rideaux, spokesperson for LITE. "We create a virtual environment for them where they actually get to see what a rig looks like and what they'll be doing."[46]

Frank's International, a company that provides pipe handling services for oil companies, has hired LITE to develop virtual reality software programs that create scenarios on oil rigs. Virtual reality training can help eliminate some of the dangers of working with heavy machinery. "Virtual reality training is the future,"[47] says Jacke West, training director at Frank's International.

Improving Safety

Reducing accidents and improving safety in the workplace is the focus of another virtual reality program. Tactus Technologies has developed a virtual reality training program for forklift operators. Using the 3D Forklift Training simulator, employees can practice handling a variety of safety challenges. They use a system that is similar to a video game, complete with a steering wheel, joystick, and pedals to maneuver through a virtual warehouse, elevators, and other settings. On average, it takes about three to four hours to complete the forklift training simulation.

Virtual reality training has an advantage over traditional training in at least one major area. Before virtual reality, forklift operators sat through classroom instruction, videos, and demonstrations before getting into a forklift and learning on the job. "The problem is that this type of training is passive rather than interactive," says Tactus cofounder and CEO Jim Mayrose. "Companies using our product will find that they have shorter training cycles with less supervision needed and, most importantly, a safer environment."[48]

Designing Buildings

In the construction industry, virtual reality applications that allow architects and builders to design and test a structure in 3D offer many benefits. To begin, architects can use a 3D virtual model of their design to determine whether the structure is viable. Traditionally, architects used judgment and scale models to assess a structure's viability. With virtual reality applications, they can construct a virtual model of the building and simulate conditions (such as wind or earthquakes) that are likely to occur. In addition, architects can test different design options before construction begins, saving time and money, reducing the number of errors in the final building, and making the entire process more efficient.

Clients can also walk through a virtual model of a building or home to see what the building will be like when it is completed. Oliver Demangel, a designer who works for the London-based 3D imaging company IVR Nation, believes that every architect will be designing projects with 3D goggles in the near future. Using photos and plans, Demangel created a virtual model of Ty Hedfan, a house in Wales. He says that it demonstrates how virtual reality will change the way architects work. "In the Ty Hedfan demo you can open the doors and turn on the lights," he says. "You can

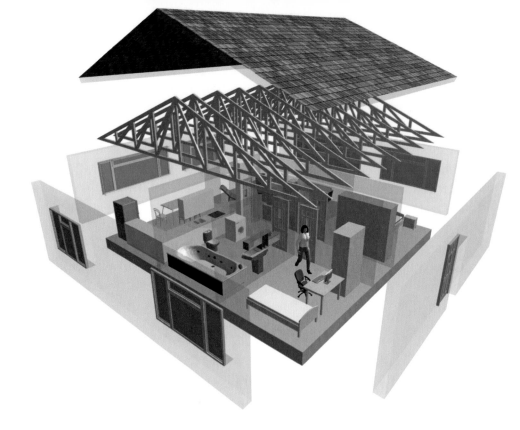

Architects can use virtual reality to test different design options before construction begins. They can even simulate strong winds and natural disasters such as earthquakes to determine the viability of a structure's design.

instantly change materials for the walls, the floor, and the position of lights. Interactivity means you can experiment with a lot of different options—design, materials, lighting, weather—very quickly." Demangel believes that architects will be using virtual reality tools within a few years to send virtual models to clients so that they can walk through the structure with 3D headsets. "We could expect an empty room with positional tracking dedicated to VR in every architecture practice, for testing new designs,"[49] he says.

Holding Virtual Meetings

Today, when employees need to attend meetings, they usually head to an office. Getting there might require them to endure traffic jams, long airport security lines, and crowded planes. Some companies use videoconferencing for meetings, but the experience is not the same as being in the same room with co-workers or clients. With virtual reality, company meetings could change dramatically. In a virtual meeting, employees would feel as though they are meeting face-to-face—without having to travel. "It could lower travel costs because meetings in a virtual world could massively exceed what we can now do with videoconferencing," says Rob Enderle, an analyst with the Enderle Group. "Done right, this could actually be better than real face-to-face in some instances."[50]

Instead of traveling to attend a business meeting in San Francisco, Jeremy Bailenson, founding director of Stanford University's Virtual Human Interaction Lab, turned to virtual reality. In the virtual meeting, he says, "I was walking around and my body was moving. . . . I was doing hand gestures, I was

literally walking around a space. And I got to walk up to someone and literally shake their hand," Bailenson says. Bailenson hopes that one day soon, employees may be able to use virtual reality to telecommute to work meetings that they do not want to attend in person. "The end goal," Bailenson says, "is to replace travel that you don't want to do. We should all travel when we want to, but let's get rid of commutes that are unnecessary and let's get rid of business meetings where you fly across the world and burn fossil fuel for an hour-long meeting. And I really believe that the software and the hardware are here. We've just now got to use it."[51]

Changing the Sales Experience

Companies are also experimenting with how virtual reality can help them connect with customers and make sales. At a time when more shoppers are purchasing online, some brands are experimenting with virtual reality as a way to lure shoppers into their stores. Stores like Ikea, Lowe's, Toms, and North Face are already using in-store experiences to make shopping more enjoyable and ultimately sell products. Shoe company Toms put virtual reality headsets into more than one hundred stores around the world in 2015. Shoppers who don the headsets become immersed in a trip to Peru, where Toms donates a pair of shoes for every pair that it sells. In the experience, viewers are immersed in a scene with panoramic views of a schoolyard while children receive boxes of donated shoes. Tyler Costin, a thirty-two-year-old from Venice, California, tried on a virtual reality headset while shopping at a California Toms store. "That's amazing," he said, swiveling in his chair to take in the 360-degree views. At one point, Costin lifted his hand to greet the students before putting it back down. He says that the experience was incredible. "It's like you're there,"[52] he says.

In 2016, Swedish home furnishings retailer Ikea launched a pilot of its Virtual Reality Kitchen, Ikea VR Experience. In this virtual reality pilot, customers enter a virtual kitchen. Using a virtual reality headset, they can explore one of three styled kitchen settings. Users can change the color of the room's cabinets and drawers with a click. In addition, they can shrink or stretch themselves to move around the kitchen and view it from different perspectives, which can reveal how it looks from the eyes of a small child or a

Selling Houses with Virtual Reality

Sotheby's International Realty has started experimenting with virtual reality to showcase multimillion-dollar luxury homes. These mansions are located in Los Angeles, California, and in New York City and Long Island, New York. Three-dimensional virtual reality scans allow potential buyers to walk through a house using a hand controller to navigate their movement. For the tour, the agent and client do not even need to be in the same physical location. For example, Sotheby's agent Matthew Hood says that he can scan a home in Venice, California, and then take a client in Asia on a virtual reality tour of that home. "I can lead a VR tour remotely and even see where the client is looking, which allows me to address things like a kitchen counter style while they're looking at it—just as I would in a real world tour," says Hood. Although virtual reality may make home buying more efficient, Hood insists that it will not entirely replace real estate agents because there are always some complications during the home-buying process that need the expertise of an agent.

Quoted in John Gaudiosi, "Now You Can Shop for Luxury Homes in Virtual Reality," *Fortune*, September 9, 2015. http://fortune.com.

A trip to a fruit market in Peru (pictured) might be one view seen by customers of companies that are using virtual reality to enhance the customer experience. Virtual reality can transport shoppers to distant locations that might be of particular interest.

tall adult. IKEA hopes that users will give feedback on the experience to help developers improve the virtual kitchen. "Virtual reality is developing quickly and in five to ten years it will be an integrated part of people's lives. We see that virtual reality will play a major role in the future of our customers. For instance, someday, it could be used to enable customers to try out a variety of home furnishing solutions before buying them,"[53] says Jesper Brodin, managing director at Ikea of Sweden.

Automotive companies are also embracing virtual reality to enhance the sales experience. In 2016 German automaker Audi unveiled its plan to bring virtual reality to its showrooms. Using an iPad, customers will select a model and then customize every element of the car, including its paint, wheels, engine, and seats.

Then they will go to a special area and put on a headset and head-phones to view their customized car in virtual reality. Customers will be able to move around the car's exterior, open its trunk and doors, look under the hood, and even sit in the driver's seat. "It's all about using technology to empower the dealer and enhance the customer experience,"[54] says Thomas Zuchtriegel, project manager with Audi Digital Retail Solutions. As far as a virtual real-ity test-drive, Zuchtriegel says that a lot of additional technology will be needed to get the experience and feel just right.

While virtual reality has been primarily used in gaming, many people are recognizing its potential across industries. With im-proved devices and platforms hitting the market in the near fu-ture, virtual reality has the potential to change the way companies do business, from improving product design to making meetings more efficient. "Like everything else, this would start as a com-petitive advantage for those early adopters," says Jeff Kagan, an independent industry analyst. "Then, over time, it will become the way we do things. At that time, companies who don't do it this new way will be behind the eight ball."[55]

Chapter 4

Military Applications

Since the early days of virtual reality, the US military has been leading the development and application of virtual reality technologies, especially for use in training. Virtual reality simulations are helping to prepare service members for life-and-death situations on the battlefield and in other dangerous conditions. Because the simulations are virtual, soldiers can practice and learn from their mistakes without getting hurt or killed. They can act out a specific scenario, such as a gun battle with the enemy in an abandoned town, without the risks of live action.

Not only is the virtual training safer but it is also less costly than traditional training approaches. The costs of ammunition and fuel needed for live training add up, and the repeated use of equipment and vehicles can wear out parts. Virtual reality training eliminates these costs and keeps equipment in top condition.

As virtual reality technology improves, the military will be able to create larger and even more realistic simulations. From pilots to snipers, virtual reality is changing the way the military prepares for war.

Flight Simulation

Flight simulations were one of the first virtual reality military applications—and one of the most successful. Flight simulators use sophisticated computer models to re-create the experience of operating an aircraft from a stationary computer. The US military uses flight simulators as part of pilot training. In these simulations, pilots practice in several scenarios, learning how to fly in battle, how to recover from unexpected emergencies or equipment failures, and coordinating air support with ground troops.

Generally, a flight simulator is designed to have the same look, controls, and layout as the cockpit of an aircraft. The flight simulator typically sits on an electronic motion base or hydraulic lift system that allows it to react to user input. When the pilot steers the aircraft, the module twists and tilts, giving the user haptic feedback which he or she can feel. Some flight simulators are completely enclosed, but others are a series of computer monitors.

At Luke Air Force Base in Arizona, US fighter pilots train to operate F-35 Lightning II fighter aircraft on flight simulators. "We are using game engines and the actual plane's software and controls to create a simulated environment that feels and looks real," says Mike Luntz, Lockheed Martin's F-35 Training System director. "Think about the F-35 simulator as a snow globe with the pilot in the middle. The pilot is completely immersed in a virtual world." More than 70 percent of the F-35 pilot training is done on a simulator before the pilot even enters the aircraft's cockpit. "Pilots often share that the F-35 simulator is so realistic they forget they aren't actually flying," says Luntz. "The simulator uses the same software as the jets themselves, and that makes a major difference for training realism and effectiveness."[56]

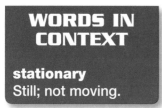

Because of space and other limitations, it is difficult to challenge pilots in all of the F-35's capabilities in real life. For example, US Air Force bases cannot fire live missiles into the sky simply for pilot training. However, in a virtual environment, trainers can challenge pilots with many different scenarios. "In the simulator, we can turn on all of the bells and whistles to provide pilots with the range of training required to maximize the F-35," says Luntz. "We can put the pilots in extremely challenging missions so that they can react more quickly and confidently during the missions they are asked to take on to defend freedom all around the world."[57] In addition to combat situations, pilots train for air refueling and shipboard landings.

With virtual reality, pilots can make mistakes in a safe environment, without having to worry about crashing an expensive plane or getting hurt. The experience makes them better prepared to handle missions and emergency situations before they even step into a real plane. Lieutenant Colonel Christine Mau completed

Flight simulators, similar to the one shown here, are being used to train military pilots. Using virtual reality flight simulators, pilots can practice flying through active war zones, coordinating with ground troops, and recovering from equipment failures.

fourteen virtual training missions on the F-35 before she rose in the air on her first F-35 training flight. She says that the virtual simulator prepared her for the real thing. "It wasn't until I was taxiing to the runway that it really struck me that I was on my own in the jet," Mau says. "I had a chase aircraft, but there was no weapons system officer or instructor pilot sitting behind me, and no one in my ear like in simulators. The training missions in the simulator prepare you very well, so you're ready for that flight,"[58] says Mau.

Ground and Water Vehicle Simulation

The military also uses virtual reality simulators to train soldiers in the operation of ground and water vehicles. The US Army uses this technology to teach soldiers how to drive specialized vehicles like tanks or the heavy-armored Stryker vehicle in a variety of conditions. Soldiers can practice handling a vehicle in bad weather, difficult terrain, or even in urban environments. Connected by a

Battlefield Visualization

Knowing the conditions and environment that service members will face is a critical part of a military commander's job. It is essential for making strategic and well-informed decisions to complete missions and keep personnel out of harm's way. For this reason, the military is also exploring the use of virtual reality to help commanders with battlefield decision making. A virtual reality workbench display can create a realistic 3D representation of a battlefield. Officers put on virtual reality headsets, which create an illusion of depth, and look at the maps and other images projected on the workbench display. Multiple users wearing headsets can see the same display simultaneously. The display gives military commanders an accurate view of the environment and battle situations. They can quickly identify potential problems, such as bottlenecks or places for a hidden enemy attack, and create alternate strategies.

network to other simulators, trainees can even participate together in complicated war games.

Virtual reality simulations are also used by the US Navy for training submarine crews. Some submarine simulators are mounted on pneumatic arms that tilt the simulator's platform to give the trainees a realistic sense of the submarine diving and surfacing. The navy has also created virtual environments that replicate the bridge of a large navy ship, with dozens of computer monitors. In this type of simulator, navy bridge teams train together, tackling various scenarios and learning how to work together.

Battlefield Simulation

Virtual environments can also prepare service members for what they will face on the battlefield. Exposing recruits to battlefield scenarios can make them better able to handle stressful situations in the real world. Military officials and video game studios have partnered to create immersive virtual reality scenarios that place military personnel in a variety of combat situations and environments involving buildings, enemy fighters, and hazards such as improvised explosive devices (IEDs).

The army began using one such system in 2012. The Dismounted Soldier Training System (DSTS) allows soldiers to train for combat situations within a virtual environment. Virtual interactions involve the use of weapons and other combat equipment, arm and hand signals to communicate with team members, and leaning around or under an obstacle such as a wall or vehicle. It also simulates the movement of ground vehicles, aircraft, and weaponry. A 360-degree surround sound system envelops the soldiers in the sounds of war and re-creates climate factors such as rain, wind, and storms. Soldiers using this training system receive immediate feedback on their performance so that they can improve the next time.

At the Camp Atterbury Joint Maneuver Training Center in Indiana, nine soldiers put on goggles, strap sensors to their arms and legs, and carry a computer-enhanced weapon system. In a warehouse, the soldiers prepare to virtually train using the DSTS. Each soldier stands on a 4-foot (1.2 m) rubber pad. They can see and hear the virtual environment and communicate with other members of the squad. Practicing a building-entry exercise, the nine soldiers encounter and react to enemy fire. When one member goes down, the team has to quickly adjust on the spot and continue the mission. "A soldier uses his body to perform maneuvers, such as walking or throwing a hand grenade, by physically making those actions. The sensors capture the soldier's movements, and those movements are translated to control the soldier's avatar within the simulation,"[59] explains Matthew Roell, a DSTS operator.

After the team completes the mission, the system operators load a new virtual environment. In the next mission, the squad faces enemy fire and a mortar attack. They call for close air support and successfully enter the building. "We can create any simulated operational environment, desert or jungle, with any weapons system and any number of enemy forces with a few key strokes,"[60] says Brandon Roell, a DSTS technician. After the training is complete, the DSTS provides a complete digital playback of

US soldiers at Camp Atterbury in Indiana have already begun training for war on lifelike virtual battlefields that subject them to a variety of combat situations and environments. A screen shot from one of the virtual reality programs is pictured.

the training session from different points of view. Trainers can use the playback to give feedback on each soldier's performance as well as on the entire squad's.

Camp Atterbury trainers are also using another virtual reality tool. This one is called Engagement Skills Trainer 2000, and it is used to teach soldiers how to fire weapons. The system tracks progress as soldiers fire their weapons multiple times. The system helps improve accuracy while also giving soldiers experience handling several types of weapons without wasting ammunition. "It feels like firing a real M4 [assault rifle]. When firing on the zero range, the target is brought up on the screen to show the results. If the shot group is tight, the computer makes the adjustment to zero the weapon. If the shot group is not tight, it gives us mentor/ trainers the opportunity to observe the soldiers to make sure they are practicing good, basic marksmanship techniques,"[61] says Sergeant First Class Robert P. Braun.

Medic Training

Military medics are also using virtual reality to train for stressful and dangerous battlefield conditions. When called, the medic must be ready to rush across the battlefield to treat wounded service members. In virtual reality, medics can train and prepare for these real-life situations. In one battlefield scenario, the medic trainee kneels next to a fallen soldier. The soldier's blood pressure has dropped very low, and his pulse is beating weakly. The soldier's foot is gone, and what is left of his leg is a mess of splintered bone and flesh. As the medic fumbles to secure a tourniquet on the soldier's leg, he or she can hear the sounds of fighting all around. Yet the medic is not actually in danger; he or she is practicing these skills in a virtual environment.

The virtual environment that the medic is using is being developed by Plextek, a British electronics design company that has been making medic training simulations for the British government. Before medics are called to an actual battlefield, Plextek hopes that its virtual reality simulation will give them

a sense of what it is like to experience battlefield stress. "When someone's been hit by an explosive and the foot's been blown off, you want to make sure the pallor on the face is correct; you want to stop the bleeding," says Collette Johnson, a manager at Plextek. "We wanted to make sure it was life-like, the breathing, the way you can put a tourniquet on. We needed something that made people feel like they were in the situation."[62] Plextek's battlefield simulation takes place in a generic desert town and gives trainees a sense of what the battlefield will be like before they leave the base. Wearing an Oculus Rift headset, the trainee is transported into an immersive, realistic battlefield environment. The headset uses head-tracking technology so that soldiers can look around their environment. A hand-held controller allows them to move through the battleground and help the wounded. They are tasked with providing medical care on the frontlines while under fire. Multiple trainees can train together in the same setting, and a controller can manipulate the condition of the wounded and the environment. They can put the patient in more distress or simulate enemy sniper attacks. After the training simulation is completed, trainees receive a recording and evaluation of their performance.

Johnson says that her team works hard to make sure that the simulation is as realistic as possible in order to assess how medic trainees will react to the stress of the battlefield. In future versions, the team will be making battle wounds look more realistic by superimposing photographs on top of them. "Some of the people who had this experience said, 'This is really real.' I think they were expecting much more of a gaming environment," Johnson says. "And that was a real positive for us, because we didn't want it to feel like a game."[63] Plextek believes that the simulation software could be used in the future for even more scenarios, including nonmilitary disaster relief and medical training.

Urban Combat Training

US ground troops may soon use virtual reality simulations to train for fighting in urban locations. These locations, including big cities surrounded by large shantytowns, are very tricky to navigate. "We are going to be on the top floor of a skyscraper evacuating civilians and helping people. The middle floor, we might be detaining really bad people that we've caught. On the first floor we will be down there killing them," says Brigadier General Julian Alford, commander of the Marine Corps Warfighting Laboratory. "At the same time they will be getting away through the subway or subterrain. How do we train to fight that? Because it is coming."

Training for a war amid skyscrapers is difficult. It is too expensive to build a twenty-story building to use for practice. With virtual reality and head-mounted displays, troops can navigate through towering buildings, vehicles, explosions, and bombs, feeling the sensation and learning how to approach a mission in the urban environment.

Quoted in Christopher Harress, "US Military Urban Combat Training: Virtual Reality Could Be Used to Prepare for Fighting in Megacities," *International Business Times,* December 28, 2015. www.ibtimes.com.

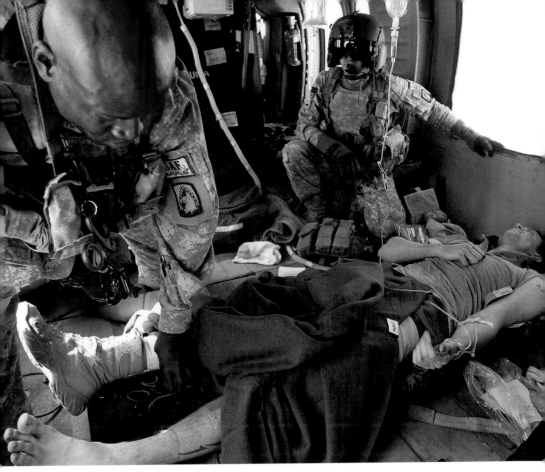

A US Army flight medic tends to a US Marine wounded by sniper fire in Afghanistan. Virtual reality training is helping military medics prepare for working in the stressful and dangerous environments of active battlefields.

The Next Generation of Virtual Reality Training

In the future, the military use of virtual reality is expected to be bigger and better. Military designers are working on a new generation of virtual reality training tools customized for each service member's needs. The idea is to create tools that can be accessed from anywhere in the world. "The next capability will be a leader-focused, soldier-centric capability that immerses a soldier, wherever they are at the point of training, in a synthetic environment, that allows us to tailor that environment to the demands of the leader,"[64] says Colonel David S. Cannon of the Combined Arms Center. Army officials expect that these new virtual reality tools could be ready for use by 2023. The virtual reality training tools will live on a cloud-based network so that soldiers can participate in training exercises no matter where they are stationed. For example, a soldier in Germany could train alongside a soldier in California.

Cannon pictures a customizable training environment where soldiers wear 3D goggles and are fully immersed in realistic scenarios that require the use of real-life skills such as assembling and disassembling weapons. In the virtual world, soldiers "will get the repetitions they need. . . . And we make it fun for them. We make it so they compete against their buddies. So by the time they get to the range, they enter at a higher skill level than we would have if we had put them on a bus and took them to the range and started firing,"[65] says Cannon.

The logistics of integrating different virtual reality simulators presents challenges for the military. Most of the virtual reality tools already in use were developed at different times, with different software, and by different companies. Getting all of these tools to work together is not easy. For example, two simulators might interpret the same terrain differently when connected. Improvements in network architecture and other technology might help smooth some of these differences. The military's long-term goal is to be able to connect all of its simulators and create an integrated training environment for large numbers of personnel. Battalion staffs would train in a battle command simulation while platoons and squads carry out the ordered missions through linked simulators.

Although virtual reality may help the military train more efficiently, it will never completely replace live training. Yet it will continue to play an increasingly important role, allowing service members to improve their skills before they hit a live environment.

Chapter 5

Medical Breakthroughs

Phantom limb pain is a common problem for amputees. It is the sensation of pain in an area where a limb has been amputated. About 70 percent of amputees experience phantom limb pain, which is sometimes intense and debilitating. Although the source of the pain is unknown, doctors suspect that it may come from nerve endings at the amputation site. The nerve endings may be sending messages to the brain, tricking it into thinking that the limb is still there and feeling pain. Current treatments include drugs, hypnosis, and mirror therapy in which patients use mirrors to trick the brain into thinking the missing limb is intact.

Researchers at Chalmers University of Technology in Sweden are testing a virtual reality therapy for phantom limb pain. When amputees played a virtual reality computer game that allows them to move a virtual limb, they reported less pain. One of the test subjects was Ture Johanson, seventy-three, who lost half of his right arm in a car accident forty-eight years ago. Johanson has been experiencing significant phantom limb pain for years. Electrodes placed on the stump of Johanson's arm recorded muscle signals to control a virtual arm and wrist that steered a car in a virtual racing game. After using the virtual game regularly at home, Johanson reported that his pain decreased dramatically. He was able to sleep through the night without waking and experienced some completely pain-free periods. "He was extremely happy, as you could imagine. He hadn't used his arm in 48 years, and that's exactly why we do the research. It's truly rewarding to see it working like this,"[66] says Max Ortiz Catalan, a researcher at Chalmers University.

Virtual reality technology has been embraced by other members of the medical profession. Doctors and nurses in some hospitals are using virtual reality systems to practice surgeries and other procedures, improving their skills without risk to patients.

Helping Kids with Autism

Professors at the University of Texas at Dallas created a virtual training program to help kids with autism work on social skills. Their virtual town, Brainville, features a school, bookstore, movie theater, and apartment building. While in Brainville, children with autism spectrum disorders practice social interaction in a safe, controlled environment. The skills they practice in the virtual world can be applied to real-life interactions with friends and family.

To enter Brainville, users put on a set of headphones and sit in front of a computer screen. The screen shows images similar to those in a first-person video game. The patient navigates the virtual town and interacts with other characters operated by a clinician, who sits behind a wall with a one-way mirror. Facial recognition software reproduces expressions on the clinician's face onto the virtual characters' faces. Josh McCombs, who has been diagnosed with Asperger's, has participated in several weeks of Brainville sessions. His mother, Jessica, says that Brainville has been one of his most helpful therapies. "It could present real-life play-by-play scenarios, where the examples could be programmed and the reactions could be programmed," says Jessica. "So you could talk about deeper things, like if somebody is aloof or if somebody is frustrated. These are very nuanced kinds of social experiences that are hard to talk about without actually experiencing. Brainville allows them to do that in a real safe, controlled environment with someone coaching them as it's happening—because you can't be there to coach if it's happening on the playground."

Quoted in Dan Koller, "Virtual Technology Teaches Kids with Autism to Interact Socially," *DFW Child,* November 2015. www.dfwchild.com.

Researchers are also developing ways to use virtual reality to treat and diagnose patients for a multitude of conditions. According to research and consulting firm Industry ARC, the demand for virtual reality for health care applications is strong and is projected to generate $2.54 billion globally by 2020.

Virtual Training

Virtual reality technology is proving to be a useful tool for training doctors, nurses, and other medical specialists. It allows them to practice new skills and techniques as many times as needed without risking the health of patients. One company, Next Galaxy Corporation, has partnered with Nicklaus Children's Hospital in Florida to develop virtual reality medical simulations for a variety of common medical procedures, including cardiopulmonary resuscitation (CPR), intubating airways, intravenous (IV) insertion, and wound care. The Next Galaxy software uses force feedback technology in which the simulation pushes back so that trainees can feel when they are doing something wrong in the procedure. In this way, medical students can learn from both visual and physical feedback when practicing a skill.

Nursing students are also beginning to use virtual reality in their training. At Boise State University (BSU) in Idaho, nursing students can play a virtual reality game that allows them to practice complex medical procedures over and over again. The game was created by a team of nursing and gaming professionals. "We call it deliberate practice—the idea that you can't really learn a procedure unless you're able to do it repeatedly and build up that muscle memory," says Ann Butt, a clinical nursing professor at BSU. "Unfortunately, what you often see in medical and nursing school is students are only able to practice a procedure once or twice and that's expected to be sufficient. This system will change that."[67]

To use the system, nursing students don sensory gloves and virtual reality goggles to enter a virtual environment where they complete tasks such as inserting catheters and sterilizing equipment. They receive a score based on their proficiency. "Because it was presented like a game, it was fun and easier to learn," says Katrina Wuori, a senior nursing student at BSU. "It sounds funny but you can compete for how accurately and quickly you can insert a catheter compared to another student, and it seemed like that competition made everyone try harder."[68] The virtual simulations are also significantly less expensive than traditional training mannequins that cost between $15,000 and $64,000. In comparison, the virtual reality technology costs

> **WORDS IN CONTEXT**
>
> **force feedback**
> When a virtual simulation pushes back against a user's tools so that he or she can feel the effects of the motion and mistakes.

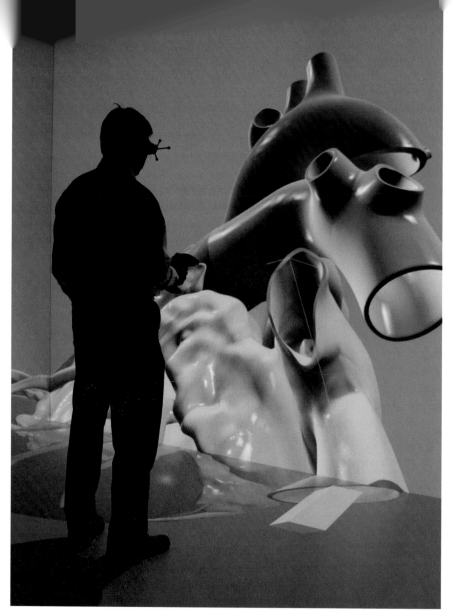

A realistic 3D simulation of a human heart (pictured) allows doctors and others to place themselves inside the heart to better understand how to treat cardiovascular disease. Researchers are applying advances in virtual reality technology to the diagnosis and treatment of many illnesses.

about $5,000 per game. The system's creators hope to develop more simulation games, including some that would allow nursing and medical students to work on procedures together.

Researchers have found that medical staff who participate in virtual training are more likely to retain the information they learn.

At Miami Children's Health System, CEO Narendra Kini reported that when tested a year later, participants in virtual reality training retained 80 percent of the information presented as compared to 20 percent retention for staff who trained using traditional methods. Kini suggests that this increased retention may happen because the virtual participants created actual memories of performing the tasks during training. "The level of understanding through VR is great because humans are primarily visual and VR is a visual format," says Kini. "We believe that there are numerous opportunities where repetitive training and skill set maintenance are critical for outcomes. Since there are not enough patients in many cases to maintain these skill sets, virtual reality is a real addition to the arsenal. Imagine also scenarios where we need to practice for accreditation and/or compliance. In these situations virtual reality is a god-send."[69]

Surgery Simulation

In the same way that pilots train with flight simulators before getting into the cockpit of a plane, future surgeons might one day routinely train with virtual reality surgical simulators. In these simulations, doctors will be able to plan and practice complex surgical operations, getting hands-on experience before actually operating on a patient.

Virtual reality surgical simulation puts surgeons into a virtual operating room, where they operate on a virtual patient in real time. At the Montreal Neurological Institute at McGill University in Canada, surgical residents are training with one of the most advanced virtual reality brain surgery tools in the world. Built in 2012, the NeuroTouch Cranio enables surgical residents to perform complex surgeries without having to cut into real patients. In the simulator, doctors hold virtual surgical tools that provide artificial sensations similar to real life. For instance, a screen might display a high-definition simulation of a tumor and how it responds to the tools. The simulator lets surgical residents learn by feel and sight as they practice a surgery to remove a brain tumor. The simulator can also identify which medical students have acquired excellent surgical skills and which need additional training.

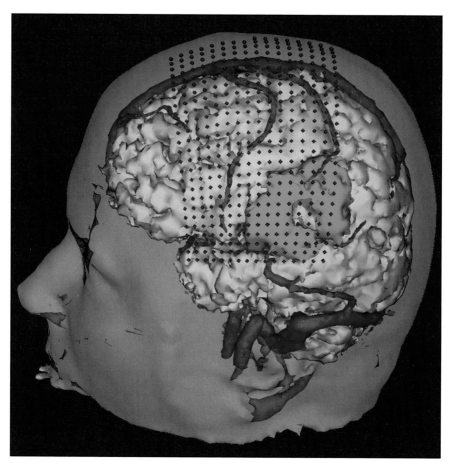

A colored 3D scan reveals a tumor (green) and blood vessels (red) in a patient's brain. Images like this are used in 3D virtual-reality-assisted surgery to help plan and carry out removal of tumors in highly sensitive areas such as the brain.

In addition to training medical students, virtual reality tools are helping surgeons prepare for complex surgeries. At the University of California, Los Angeles (UCLA), neurosurgeons are donning virtual reality headsets to go inside patients' brains. "It's just amazing to see every little opening in the skull where a nerve goes through," says Neil Martin, chairman of UCLA's Department of Neurosurgery. "I'm virtually inside the skull of the patient walking around, floating around." Martin is developing the technology along with Surgical Theater, a virtual reality company. Neurosurgeons often operate on patients with tumors and aneurysms that are dangerously close to areas of the brain that control movement and language.

One wrong move and a patient can become permanently brain damaged. Using virtual reality technology, neurosurgeons would be able to practice before the surgery. Even during the surgery, a neurosurgeon could put the virtual reality headset on to remind himself of where and when to expect challenging sections of the surgery. "On the image, I can see the carotid artery going through the margin of the tumor. . . . Rather than have that all of a sudden appear as I'm removing [the] tumor, I'll know exactly when I'm going to encounter it," says Martin. "That is a big improvement."[70] Martin believes that this technology will be a significant benefit to patients by helping doctors operate faster and with more success.

Improving Diagnosis

Virtual reality is not limited to surgical applications in medicine. It can also be used to help doctors diagnose various illnesses and disorders. At Toronto Western Hospital in Canada, researchers are studying how Oculus Rift can be used to detect early changes in peripheral vision for glaucoma patients. Glaucoma is a disease that damages the eye's optic nerve and can gradually lead to blindness. But blindness can often be prevented through early detection and treatment. One of the first symptoms of glaucoma is blind spots in a patient's peripheral vision. By using the Oculus Rift headset to detect these changes in peripheral vision, doctors can treat patients in the early stages of the disease.

Researchers at the University of Bonn in Germany believe they can use virtual reality technology to identify early signs of Alzheimer's disease in people aged eighteen to thirty. The researchers built a virtual space with blue sky, mountains, and a grass floor. Across the virtual landscape, they scattered everyday objects. Study participants were instructed to walk around the virtual landscape and collect objects and then later return them to the same place. As the participants maneuvered the virtual landscape, researchers monitored their brain activity with magnetic resonance imaging. They discovered that participants

Treating Addiction

Virtual reality may one day be used to help people with drug and alcohol addictions. In South Korea, a study of ten patients with alcohol dependence has shown promise. First, participants went through a week-long detoxification. This was followed by twice-weekly virtual reality sessions for five weeks. During each session, participants worked through three scenarios. The first scenario relaxed them, and the second was designed to trigger alcohol cravings by putting participants in situations where other people drank alcohol. The third scenario transported participants to a room where people were throwing up from alcohol. In addition, the participants consumed a vomit-tasting drink during the third scenario. Researchers found that after repeated sessions, the areas of the brain sensitive to alcohol showed changes. Before therapy, the alcohol-dependent participants showed more activity in the limbic systems of the brain, areas connected to emotions and behavior, as compared to people without alcohol dependence. After five weeks of virtual reality therapy, scans showed that the activity in these brain areas decreased for the alcohol-dependent participants. Subjects also reported reduced alcohol cravings after therapy. Although the results appear promising, researchers say that more studies need to be done to determine the long-term effectiveness of virtual reality as an addiction treatment.

with a higher genetic likelihood of developing Alzheimer's had different brain activity during the simulation than participants with a lower genetic risk. "The at-risk group showed a different brain signal many decades before the onset of the disease, and they navigated differently in a virtual environment,"[71] the researchers reported. Specifically, the participants at higher risk of developing Alzheimer's had less activity in the network of cells in the brain that are used for navigation and memory tasks (called grid cells). The researchers noted that the participants did not perform worse in the virtual tasks; they just used a different part of their brain. They were more likely to use the hippocampus, the part of the brain linked to memory and emotion, than the grid cells. This difference in brain activity could lead to better understanding of why people with Alzheimer's disease have trouble navigating the world and open new avenues for potential treatments. "Although we don't know whether young people in this study will go on to develop Alzheimer's, characterising early brain changes associated with genetic risk factors is important to help researchers better understand why some people may be more susceptible to the disease later in life,"[72] says Laura Pipps, a spokeswoman with Alzheimer's Research, a nonprofit organization in the United Kingdom.

Treating Phobias and PTSD

Virtual reality can also be used to help people who suffer from phobias. For these people, something as simple as a plane or a crowded room can trigger an intense and irrational fear response. Mental health professionals have begun using virtual reality to treat patients with phobias and help them overcome their fears. To date, virtual reality has primarily been used for exposure therapy, a form of behavior therapy that gradually exposes patients to the situation or objects that trigger their phobia and the feelings of anxiety that it causes. When people are afraid of something, they tend to avoid it. Although this may help in the short-term, over time, avoidance can make the fear worse. Exposure therapy creates a safe environment where patients are exposed to their fears. Over time, repeated exposures can reduce fear and avoidance. In addition, mental health professionals also use cognitive behavioral therapy to teach patients strategies for dealing with situations that cause stress and anxiety.

WORDS IN CONTEXT

exposure therapy
A form of behavior therapy that gradually exposes patients to their fears.

With virtual reality, a mental health professional can create a scene that triggers a patient's fear or anxiety. They can put them on a virtual plane or in a room with a feared object. Researchers have treated people with arachnophobia—the fear of spiders—by exposing them to virtual spiders and having them touch fake spiders.

Virtual reality is also being used to treat patients with post-traumatic stress disorder (PTSD). PTSD is a disorder that can develop when a person lives through a shocking, scary, or dangerous event. Although many people who experience these kinds of events feel some leftover anxiety and fear, they eventually recover

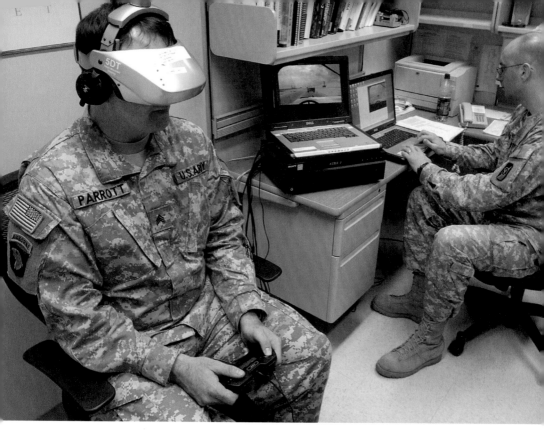

As part of his treatment for PTSD, a US soldier uses a head-mounted viewer and handheld device to control his movements during a virtual reality simulation. Treatment includes exposing the soldier to realistic simulations of the events that brought about the PTSD.

and move on with their lives. People with PTSD, however, continue to experience flashbacks, nightmares, and anxiety for months and even years after the traumatic event. PTSD symptoms can interfere with a person's ability to function in daily life. Loud noises might trigger a soldier's memory of a battle or bomb, making it difficult for him or her to resume a civilian life. Assault victims might be paralyzed with fear after encountering a stranger on the street. For those who suffer from PTSD, overcoming fear and anxiety is an important step toward resuming a normal life.

At the Miami VA (Veterans Affairs) Healthcare System, mental health providers are using virtual reality to help veterans with PTSD. Patients put on a virtual reality headset and hold a plastic rifle and a remote to control a virtual Humvee while they maneuver a virtual combat situation. "Patients begin the session by recounting their traumatic memories in the present tense, while we document responses, anxiety levels and memories," says Pamela Slone-Fama, a Miami VA post-traumatic stress clinical team staff psychologist. "As patients are recounting, we can see what they are seeing on our screens and try to simulate the landscapes, sounds and smells they are describing." As they recall their memories, the patients also describe their feelings. After each virtual reality session, therapists work with the patients to help them work through their feelings about what they experienced. "This part of the therapy helps patients understand the events that happened to them and allows them to process the entire memory. VR sessions can be intense, so before wrapping up we always make sure the patients are ok to leave. Safety is always important,"[73] says Slone-Fama.

Breakthrough Technology

The ability to transport people into virtual worlds has existed for years in people's imaginations, books, and movies. In recent years, however, real-world technology has begun to catch up with these fictional systems, bringing virtual reality scenarios to life. With increasingly sophisticated technology, researchers are coming up with ways to use virtual reality across a variety of industries, from entertainment to medicine. As the technology continues to advance and as headsets become smaller and more responsive, even more applications will emerge. Less than twenty years ago, it was difficult to imagine how much a part of daily life mobile phones would become. Today, however, it is hard to imagine life without a mobile phone. Virtual reality holds similar promise to become the next big technology breakthrough that changes life around the world.

Source Notes

Introduction: Stepping Inside a New World

1. Quoted in Matt Wood, "Training the Next Generation of Neurosurgeons in Virtual Reality," University of Chicago Medicine, January 23, 2013. https://sciencelife.uchospitals.edu.
2. Quoted in Wood, "Training the Next Generation of Neurosurgeons in Virtual Reality."
3. Quoted in Wood, "Training the Next Generation of Neurosurgeons in Virtual Reality."
4. Quoted in John Patrick Pullen, "You Asked: How Do Virtual Reality Headsets Work?," *Time*, January 23, 2015. http://time.com.
5. Mark Zuckerberg, Facebook post, March 25, 2014. www.facebook.com.

Chapter 1: Immersive Entertainment

6. Quoted in Maria Konnikova, "Virtual Reality Gets Real: The Promises—and Pitfalls—of the Emerging Technology," *Atlantic*, October 2015. www.theatlantic.com.
7. Quoted in Tom Simonite, "Google Aims to Make VR Hardware Irrelevant Before It Even Gets Going," *MIT Technology Review,* November 3, 2015. www.technologyreview.com.
8. Quoted in Brian Mastroianni, "Oculus Rift VR Reviews Are In: Should You Buy?," CBS News, March 29, 2016. www.cbsnews.com.
9. Alex Hern, "Will 2016 Be the Year Virtual Reality Gaming Takes Off?," *Guardian,* December 28, 2015. www.theguardian.com.
10. Quoted in Hern, "Will 2016 Be the Year Virtual Reality Gaming Takes Off?"
11. Quoted in Stuart Dredge, "Oculus VR: 'Classrooms Are Broken. Kids Don't Learn the Best by Reading Books,'" *Guardian*, November 3, 2015. www.theguardian.com.

12. Quoted in Stuart Dredge, "Three Really Real Questions About the Future of Virtual Reality," *Guardian,* January 7, 2016. www.theguardian.com.

13. Quoted in Realty Today, "20th Century Fox to Release 100 Movies to Oculus Rift, so as to Bring Virtual Reality to Movies," September 28, 2015.www.realtytoday.com.

14. Quoted in Jamieson Cox, "*The Martian* VR Experience Is Out of This World," *Verge*, January 9, 2016. www.theverge.com.

15. Quoted in Lorenza Brascia and Stephanie Elam, "How Virtual Reality Could Change Moviegoing," CNN, January 28, 2016. www.cnn.com.

16. Quoted in Brascia and Elam, "How Virtual Reality Could Change Moviegoing."

17. Quoted in Stuart Dredge, "Could Virtual Reality Revolutionise Crisis-Response Filmmaking?," *Guardian,* August 13, 2015. www.theguardian.com.

18. Quoted in Dredge, "Could Virtual Reality Revolutionise Crisis-Response Filmmaking?"

19. Quoted in Robert Gray, "Fox Sports Teams with NextVR to Broadcast Live Sports in Virtual Reality," Fox News, February 17, 2016. www.foxnews.com.

20. Quoted in Dan Daley, "Fox Takes VR to Next Level at Daytona," Sports Video Group, February 23, 2016. www.sports video.org.

21. Quoted in Daley, "Fox Takes VR to Next Level at Daytona."

22. Quoted in Joseph Volpe, "Fox Pushes Virtual Reality to the Limit with 30 Minutes on Mars," Engadget, January 18, 2016. www.engadget.com.

Chapter 2: Engaging Education

23. Quoted in Joanna Duffy, "Watertown Middle School Students Experiment with Google Expeditions," Wicked Local Watertown, March 17, 2016. http://watertown.wickedlocal.com.

24. Quoted in Georgia Wells, "Virtual Reality Learns How to Get Into the Classroom," *Digits* (blog), *Wall Street Journal,* February 11, 2016. http://blogs.wsj.com.

25. Quoted in Heather Hansman, "How Can Schools Use Virtual Reality?," *Smithsonian*, February 3, 2016. www.smithsonianmag.com.
26. Quoted in Marco della Cava, "Google Rolls Out Virtual Reality Field Trips," *USA Today*, September 28, 2015. www.usatoday.com.
27. Quoted in John A. Byrne, "Harvard Business School Really Has Created the Classroom of the Future," *Fortune*, August 25, 2015. http://fortune.com.
28. Quoted in Byrne, "Harvard Business School Really Has Created the Classroom of the Future."
29. Quoted in Michelle Reis, "Could Virtual Reality Be the Next Big Thing in Education?," *Forbes*, August 27, 2014. www.forbes.com.
30. Quoted in Audrey Breen, "A Virtual Reality Classroom Simulator for Teachers in Training," Phys.org, April 19, 2016. http://phys.org.
31. Quoted in Breen, "A Virtual Reality Classroom Simulator for Teachers in Training."
32. Quoted in Greg Watry, "A Simulation's Teaching Moment," *R&D Magazine,* April 19, 2016. www.rdmag.com.
33. Quoted in Breen, "A Virtual Reality Classroom Simulator for Teachers in Training."
34. Quoted in Kyle Nofuente, "Virtual Reality and the Future of Museum Tours: Using Oculus Rift to Dream with Disney and Dali," Tech Times, January 27, 2016. www.techtimes.com.
35. Quoted in Jeff Beer, "Go Inside the Work of Salvador Dali with Surreal New Virtual Reality Experience," *Fast Company*, January 20, 2016. www.fastcocreate.com.
36. Quoted in Maev Kennedy, "British Museum Uses Virtual Reality to Transport Visitors to the Bronze Age," *Guardian,* August 4, 2015. www.theguardian.com.
37. Quoted in John Gaudiosi, "These Two School Districts Are Teaching Through Virtual Reality," *Fortune*, February 25, 2016. http://fortune.com.

Chapter 3: Virtual Reality in Business

38. Quoted in Ashley Rodriguez, "Outdoor-Apparel Brand Merrell Uses Virtual Reality to Refresh Brand," *Advertising Age*, February 6, 2015. http://adage.com.

39. Quoted in Rodriguez, "Outdoor-Apparel Brand Merrell Uses Virtual Reality to Refresh Brand."

40. Quoted in Rodriguez, "Outdoor-Apparel Brand Merrell Uses Virtual Reality to Refresh Brand."

41. Quoted in Kieron Monks, "A Whole New World: 5 Ways Virtual Reality Can Transform Business," CNN, November 25, 2014. http://edition.cnn.com.

42. Quoted in Reis, "Could Virtual Reality Be the Next Big Thing in Education?"

43. Quoted in Wayne Grayson, "How Caterpillar Is Developing Virtual and Augmented Reality to Design and Service Heavy Equipment," *Equipment World,* October 22, 2015. www.equipmentworld.com.

44. Quoted in Monks, "A Whole New World."

45. Quoted in Kyle Rothenberg, "Oil Companies Tap Virtual Technology to Train Workers," Fox News, November 10, 2014. www.foxnews.com.

46. Quoted in Rothenberg, "Oil Companies Tap Virtual Technology to Train Workers."

47. Quoted in Rothenberg, "Oil Companies Tap Virtual Technology to Train Workers."

48. Quoted in *Occupational Health & Safety Online*, "Virtual Reality Training Program Created for Forklift Operators," March 11, 2013. https://ohsonline.com.

49. Quoted in *Dezeen*, "Virtual Reality Will Be 'More Powerful than Cocaine,'" April 27, 2015. www.dezeen.com.

50. Quoted in Sharon Gaudin, "5 Ways to Use Virtual Reality in the Enterprise," Computerworld, March 27, 2015. www.computerworld.com.

51. Quoted in Elizabeth Shockman, "How Advances in Virtual Reality Will Change How We Work and Communicate," Public Radio International, March 14, 2016. www.pri.org.

52. Quoted in Shan Li, "How Retail Stores Are Using Virtual Reality to Make Shopping More Fun," *Los Angeles Times*, April 10, 2016. www.latimes.com.
53. Quoted in Ikea, "Ikea Launches Pilot Virtual Reality (VR) Kitchen Experience for HTC Vive on Steam," April 4, 2016. www.ikea.com.
54. Quoted in John Gaudiosi, "Audi Drives Virtual Reality Showroom with HTC Vibe," *Fortune*, January 8, 2016. www.fortune.com.
55. Quoted in Gaudin, "5 Ways to Use Virtual Reality in the Enterprise."

Chapter 4: Military Applications

56. Quoted in Lockheed Martin, "Video Games Get Serious: Why More Time in the Simulator Equals Better Training," May 18, 2015. http://lockheedmartin.com.
57. Quoted in Lockheed Martin, "Video Games Get Serious."
58. Quoted in Lockheed Martin, "Video Games Get Serious."
59. Quoted in Penny Zamora, "Virtual Training Puts the 'Real' in Realistic Environment," US Army, March 4, 2013. www.army.mil.
60. Quoted in Zamora, "Virtual Training Puts the 'Real' in Realistic Environment."
61. Quoted in Zamora, "Virtual Training Puts the 'Real' in Realistic Environment."
62. Quoted in Sydney Brownstone, "Medics Prepare for Battlefield Trauma in Oculus Rift, Without Leaving Their Chair," *Fast Company,* July 14, 2014. www.fastcoexist.com.
63. Quoted in Brownstone, "Medics Prepare for Battlefield Trauma in Oculus Rift, Without Leaving Their Chair."
64. Quoted in C. Todd Lopez, "Center Shows Glimpse of Next-Generation Synthetic Training," US Army, April 7, 2015. www.army.mil.
65. Quoted in Mark Pomerleau, "Army Outlines Plans for the Next-Generation of Virtual Training," Defense Systems, April 13, 2015. https://defensesystems.com.

Chapter 5: Medical Breakthroughs

66. Quoted in Mary-Ann Russon, "Phantom Limb Pain Can Be Treated Using Virtual Reality," *International Business Times,* February 27, 2014. www.ibtimes.co.uk.

67. Quoted in Brian Zinnerman, "Boise State Creates Virtual Reality Program to Train Nursing Students," *Becker's Hospital Review,* April 25, 2016. www.beckershospitalreview.com.

68. Quoted in Zinnerman, "Boise State Creates Virtual Reality Program."

69. Quoted in John Gaudiosi, "Here's Why Hospitals Are Using Virtual Reality to Train Staff," *Fortune*, August 17, 2015. http://fortune.com.

70. Quoted in CBS News, "Latest Tool for Neurosurgeons: Virtual Reality Headsets," May 4, 2015. www.cbsnews.com.

71. Quoted in Cara McGoogan, "VR Test Could Diagnose Very Early Onset Alzheimer's," *Wired*, October 23, 2015. www.wired.co.uk.

72. Quoted in McGoogan, "VR Test Could Diagnose Very Early Onset Alzheimer's."

73. Quoted in US Department of Veterans Affairs, "Miami VA Using Virtual Reality to Treat PTSD," *VAntage Point* (blog), December 3, 2015. www.blogs.va.gov.

For Further Research

Books

Bradley Austin Davis, Karen Bryla, and Alex Benton, *Oculus Rift in Action*. Greenwich, CT: Manning, 2015.

Tony Parisi, *Learning Virtual Reality: Developing Immersive Experiences and Applications for Desktop, Web, and Mobile*. Sebastopol, CA: O'Reilly Media, 2016.

John Perritano, *Virtual Reality*. Costa Mesa, CA: Saddleback Educational, 2015.

Don Rauf, *Virtual Reality*. New York: Rosen, 2016.

Chris Woodford, *Cool Stuff Exploded: Get Inside Modern Technology*. New York: Dorling Kindersley, 2011.

Internet Sources

Stuart Dredge, "Three Really Real Questions About the Future of Virtual Reality," *Guardian,* January 7, 2016. www.theguardian.com /technology/2016/jan/07/virtual-reality-future-oculus-rift-virtual reality.

Maria Konnikova, "Virtual Reality Gets Real: The Promises—and Pitfalls—of the Emerging Technology," *Atlantic*, October 2015. www.theatlantic.com/magazine/archive/2015/10/virtual-reality -gets-real/403225.

John Patrick Pullen, "You Asked: How Do Virtual Reality Headsets Work?," *Time*, January 23, 2015. http://time.com/3679652 /virtual-reality-headsets-how-work.

Peter Rubin, "The Inside Story of Oculus Rift and How Virtual Reality Became Reality," *Wired*, May 20, 2014. www.wired.com /2014/05/oculus-rift-4.

Knvul Sheikh, "Beyond Gaming: 10 Other Fascinating Uses for Virtual-Reality Tech," Live Science, January 19, 2016. www.live science.com/53392-virtual-reality-tech-uses-beyond-gaming .html.

Elizabeth Shockman, "How Advances in Virtual Reality Will Change How We Work and Communicate," Public Radio International, March 14, 2016. www.pri.org/stories/2016-03-14/how -advances-virtual-reality-will-change-how-we-work-and-com municate.

Jonathan Strickland, "How Virtual Reality Works," HowStuffWorks. http://electronics.howstuffworks.com/gadgets/other-gadgets /virtual-reality.htm.

Websites

Oculus (www.oculus.com). The creator of the Oculus Rift headset, this company is on the cutting edge of virtual technology.

Virtual Reality Society (www.vrs.org.uk). This website offers a variety of informational articles about virtual reality, how it works, and its applications.

Index

Picture Credits

About the Author

Carla Mooney is the author of many books for young adults and children. She lives in Pittsburgh, Pennsylvania, with her husband and three children.